W9-AJP-886

MONTANA

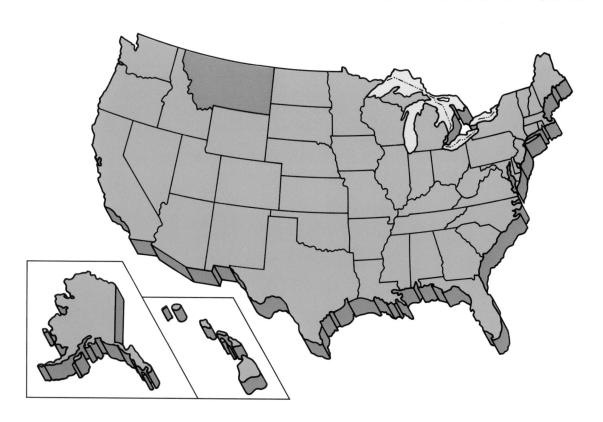

MONTANA

Rita C. LaDoux

Lerner Publications Company

This book is available in two editions:
Library binding by Lerner Publications Company
Soft cover by First Avenue Editions, 1997
241 First Avenue North
Minneapolis, MN 55401
ISBN: 0-8225-2714-6 (lib. bdg.)
ISBN: 0-8225-9782-9 (pbk.)

LIBRARY OF CONGRESS
CATALOGING-IN-PUBLICATION DATA
LaDoux, Rita.
    Montana / Rita C. LaDoux.
      p.   cm. — (Hello USA)
    Includes index.
    Summary: Introduces the history, geography,
people, industries, and other highlights of
Montana.
    ISBN 0-8225-2714-6 (lib. bdg.)
    1. Montana—Juvenile literature.
[1. Montana.] I. Title. II. Series.
F731.3.L34   1991
978.6—dc20   91-14445

Cover photograph by Gerry
Lemmo.

The glossary that begins on
page 69 gives definitions of
words shown in **bold type** in
the text.

Manufactured in the United States of America
2 3 4 5 6 7 8 9 10 - JR - 05 04 03 02 01 00 99 98 97

This book is printed
on acid-free, recycla-
ble paper.

Contents

Did You Know . . . ?

☐ So many dinosaur bones have been found near Ekalaka, Montana, that the town has been nicknamed Skeleton Flats.

☐ Montana's Roe River, the world's shortest river, travels only 201 feet (61 meters)—less than the length of a football field. The Roe flows out of Montana's Giant Springs, a large freshwater pool, and into the Missouri River.

☐ At Medicine Rocks in eastern Montana, Indian hunters once called on magical spirits to help the Indians catch more buffalo.

Last Chance Gulch

Last Chance Gulch, the main street in Helena, Montana, was once a gold-mining area. The valley got its name in 1864, when some miners stopped there for one last chance to find gold. They struck it big—mines in the area soon produced over $20 million in gold!

A Trip Around the State

Montana, which means "mountain" in Spanish, is many things to many people. Whether you call it the Land of Shining Mountains, the Treasure State, or the Big Sky Country, Montana is beautiful—and big. In fact, it is the fourth largest state in the country.

A snowboarder speeds down Big Mountain. Some peaks in Montana are capped with snow 10 months of the year.

9

National Park. Yellowstone National Park cuts into Montana's southwestern corner.

The state has two geographic regions, the Great Plains and the Rocky Mountains. Montana's Great Plains roll across the eastern two-thirds of the state. This grass-covered region is mostly flat.

Millions of years ago, dinosaurs lumbered through swamps that flooded a large part of the Great Plains. As the plants and animals in the swamps died, they sank to the bottom. The thick layer of decayed plants and animals was later buried by rock. Over thousands of years, the weight of the rock pressed the decayed layer into coal, one of Montana's most valuable minerals.

Stretching across the northwestern United States, Montana is neighbor to Canada, North Dakota, South Dakota, Wyoming, and Idaho. Along Montana's northwestern boundary lies Glacier

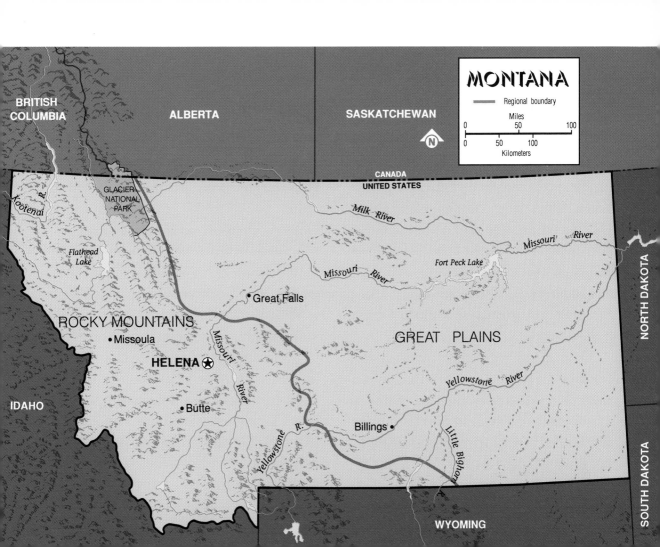

BRITISH COLUMBIA

ALBERTA

SASKATCHEWAN

MONTANA

Regional boundary

Miles
0   50   100

0   50   100
Kilometers

N

CANADA
UNITED STATES

Kootenai R.

GLACIER NATIONAL PARK

Milk River

Missouri River

Flathead Lake

Missouri River

Fort Peck Lake

NORTH DAKOTA

• Great Falls

ROCKY MOUNTAINS

GREAT PLAINS

• Missoula

Missouri River

HELENA ★

Yellowstone River

IDAHO

• Butte

Yellowstone R.

Billings •

Little Bighorn

SOUTH DAKOTA

WYOMING

The Rocky Mountains region covers the western third of Montana. This area of the state contains a small section of the Rocky Mountains, a chain that stretches from Alaska to Mexico. Within Montana's Rockies are more than 50 smaller groups of mountains, called ranges.

The Rocky Mountains were formed millions of years ago when strong pressures in the earth's crust caused western North America to buckle. Enormous blocks of rock were lifted into tall ranges. Lava, or hot liquid rock, bubbled up to the surface from deep inside the earth. The lava cooled into solid rock, some of which contained copper and gold. Later, glaciers—huge, thick sheets of slow-moving ice—carved out the peaks and valleys of the Rockies.

When rain falls on the western side of the Rockies, it collects in the Kootenai and Clark Fork rivers and flows toward the Pacific. Rain that falls on the eastern slopes of the Rockies pours into the Milk, Missouri, and Yellowstone rivers, which cut wide valleys as they wind eastward across the state.

Pasqueflowers *(above),* **bear grass** *(top right),* **and little sunflowers** *(bottom right)* **brighten Montana's wilderness.**

Besides its mighty rivers, Montana boasts Flathead Lake, the largest natural lake in the western United States. Nestled in the mountains of western Montana, Flathead was formed by glaciers, as were the many smaller lakes that dot Montana's mountain slopes.

Dams built along the Missouri and Kootenai rivers created other

large lakes, or **reservoirs,** including Fort Peck Lake. Water released from reservoirs is used to turn engines that produce electricity and for **irrigation** to water crops.

Montana has a lot of water, but some of the state gets only a little **precipitation** (rain and snow). More than 32 inches (81 centimeters) of precipitation usually falls on the western slopes of the Rockies each year. But the eastern mountains and plains are much drier, receiving about 13 inches (33 cm) per year.

In the western mountains, summers are cool and winters fairly warm. On the plains, however, summers can be scorching hot and winters bitterly cold. The state's highest temperature, recorded on the far eastern plains, was 117° F (48° C). The lowest winter temperature was a bone-chilling −70° F (−57° C).

Water from the Clark Fork River rushes through the Thompson Falls Dam.

Mountain goats *(facing page)* perch on a ledge in Glacier National Park. A frost-covered buffalo *(right)* roams a wildlife preserve.

No matter what the season, the open plains cannot stop the ever-blowing winds. The wind blows through the grasses that cover the **prairies,** or grasslands, of the Great Plains. At one time, millions of buffalo ate the prairie grasses. Now the few buffalo left in Montana graze in wildlife preserves, where they are protected from hunters. Pronghorn antelope, mule deer, and prairie dogs rely on the grasslands for food and shelter.

Grizzly bears, elk, moose, mountain goats, and bighorn sheep roam through Montana's mountains. The Rockies are forested with ash, birch, cedar, fir, pine, and spruce trees.

17

Bighorn Canyon

Montana's Story

For centuries, the people of Montana have had close ties to the land. Hunters, trappers, farmers, ranchers, miners, and loggers have made a living from the mountains and prairies of the state. Each group of people has its own story to tell. Twisted together like the strands of a rope, these stories tell the history of Montana.

Many of Montana's ranchers depend on cattle to make a living.

One story begins about 12,000 years ago with the first people to arrive in the land now called Montana. These Native Americans may have walked to North America from Asia on a narrow strip of land at what is now the Bering Strait. The Native Americans hunted buffalo and woolly mammoths, huge animals that looked like hairy elephants.

Over the next several thousand years, the world's climate changed drastically, and all the mammoths died. Hunters stalked smaller animals and gathered plants, berries, and roots to eat.

By 1600 the Native Americans had grouped into the Indian tribes we know today. In the Rockies were the Flathead, Kootenai, and Kalispel tribes, who survived by hunting and fishing. The Blackfeet, Cheyenne, Crow, Assiniboin, and Gros Ventre hunted and farmed on the Great Plains.

The life of the Plains Indians changed when Spanish explorers brought horses to America. The Plains Indians had been living in villages so they could tend to their farms. But after the 1600s, when they got horses, many Indian tribes quit farming and left their villages behind to follow and hunt roaming herds of buffalo.

Before the Plains Indians had horses, they used a travois, or sled, to carry goods.

21

The Plains Indians made many of their clothes, weapons, and tools from the hides and bones of buffalo.

Nearly everything the Plains Indians needed came from the buffalo. After a hunt, the women and older men skinned the buffalo and tanned the hides, which were used to make clothing and tepees. The Indians dried, roasted, or mixed the meat with berries and fat so that it wouldn't spoil. They carved buffalo bones into tools. And they used dried buffalo chips, or droppings, to fuel fires for cooking.

The Indians had Montana's land —and its buffalo—to themselves until 1682, when France claimed a huge tract of land in North America that included most of what is now Montana. But Europeans did not come to the region until 1803, when France sold the territory,

Louisiana Purchase

called Louisiana, to the United States in a deal called the Louisiana Purchase.

23

Eager to find out what his country had bought, U.S. president Thomas Jefferson sent explorers Meriwether Lewis and William Clark to map the new territory in 1804. Leaving from St. Louis, Missouri, the expedition traveled 1,600 miles (2,574 kilometers) up the Missouri River to what is now Montana.

In Montana, Lewis and Clark paddled canoes along the Missouri River to Three Forks, at the base of the Rocky Mountains. There, they traded their canoes to Indians for horses and rode across the mountains.

While in Montana, Lewis and Clark found many beavers. This discovery encouraged fur companies to build trading posts in the

Mountain men worked for fur companies.

region. The soft, thick pelts of beavers were in demand because they could be made into stylish hats. The fur companies sent trappers called mountain men to the

At trading posts, mountain men and Indians exchanged goods.

area. These men lived a rugged life, exploring wilderness known only to the Indians.

At trading posts set up by the fur companies, mountain men gave the Indians guns, alcohol, and tobacco in exchange for furs. In 1847 Montana's Fort Benton was built on the Missouri River. Steamboats loaded with trade goods were soon chugging up the river from St. Louis, Missouri, to the fort. From this post, the boats headed back downstream filled with furs.

White traders brought more than manufactured goods to the Indians. The traders exposed the Native Americans to European diseases such as smallpox and measles. Thousands of Indians died.

As Montana's Indian population was shrinking, waves of fortune seekers hit the region. In 1849 gold was discovered in California. Thousands of people from the eastern United States rushed west, hoping to make lots of money. But many of them found no gold in California, and they turned back to search the Rocky Mountains for the precious metal.

In 1862 prospectors discovered gold along Montana's Grasshopper Creek, and the Montana gold rush began. The gold rush brought not only settlers from east of the Mississippi River but also newcomers from other countries. Many people came from China, as well as Germany, France, Spain, and Sweden. Mining towns sprang up near gold strikes. Store owners charged high prices, and miners paid with gold dust.

The wealth also attracted outlaws, who stole from the miners, the stores, and the saloons. Prospectors and townspeople captured and hanged the criminals. In 1864 the U.S. government helped restore order by making Montana a territory of the United States. This meant that U.S. laws could be enforced in the area.

Fortune seekers used large pans to mine gold in Montana's creeks.

Montana's Frontierswomen

The women who helped settle Montana in the 1800s came from many different backgrounds. **Nellie Wibaux** *(left)* and her husband, Pierre, came from France. Their first Montana home was a log cabin with a sod roof that leaked during heavy rainstorms. **Augusta Kohrs** *(center)* and her husband, Conrad, were of German ancestry. They built a successful cattle ranching business in western Montana. And **Awbonnie Stuart** *(right),* a Shoshone Indian, ranched for 26 years with her husband, Granville, and their eleven children. Pioneer women in Montana worked hard. One day's chores might include making breakfast at 5:00 A.M., then sweeping and mopping the floors, making lunch, ironing, baking, tending the garden, mending, preparing dinner, and doing the dishes.

Cattle ranchers followed the miners to Montana. In the 1860s, cowboys began driving large herds of longhorn cattle to Montana from as far away as Texas. The ranchers sold beef to the miners and grazed their cattle on the grasslands. Montana's beef cattle industry grew as more ranchers came to the area.

In the late 1800s, cowboys brought large herds of cattle to Montana.

Roping

A Montana cowboy of the 1800s was never far from his lariat, or lasso, which he hung from the saddle on his horse. On the range, a cowboy might use his lariat to pull a cow out of the mud or to capture a cow trying to escape from the herd.

Lariats were made of braided rawhide or twisted grass. The lariat had to be stiff enough so when a cowboy sent it flying through the air the loop would stay flat and open. A lariat also had to be very strong so a big cow, which might weigh as much as 1,200 pounds (545 kilograms), couldn't break it.

The Lariat

A typical lariat was about 40 feet (12 m) long. At one end of the lariat was a little loop called a honda. The main line of the lariat passed through the honda to form a big loop. To throw a lariat took great skill. The cowboy took the big loop and the main line in his throwing hand and held the rest of the lariat in his other hand. To steer his horse, the cowboy used the last two fingers of this non-throwing hand to pull on the reins.

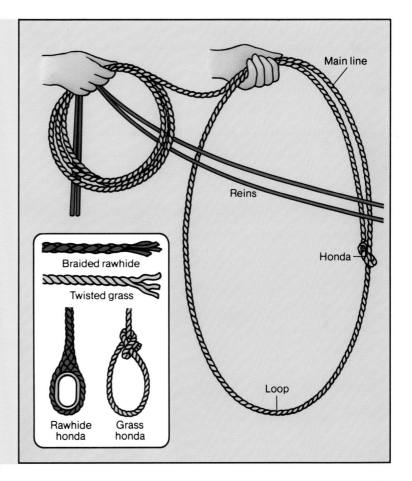

Main line

Reins

Honda

Loop

Braided rawhide

Twisted grass

Rawhide honda

Grass honda

Indians lost much of their homeland to settlers.

Cattle ranchers and other settlers lived and worked on land that had been the home of Indians. The U.S. government signed **treaties** promising the Indians that some land would be saved for them. But the government did not keep its promises.

Instead, the government took back land it had assigned to the tribes and gave the land to settlers and railroad companies. Cattle ranchers, train crews, and sport hunters killed millions of buffalo—the Indians' main source of food.

Gradually, the U.S. government forced most Indians in Montana onto **reservations**—areas of land reserved for Native Americans. The Indians were expected to give up hunting and to farm their land.

In the late 1800s, the Cree people did not have a reservation of their own. Without land, they suffered hardship for many years. In 1916 the Rocky Boy's Reservation in north central Montana was finally established for them. In the middle of this photo stands Little Bear, a Cree chief.

Some Plains Indians fought hard to keep their land. One of their most famous struggles was the Battle of the Little Bighorn. In 1876 Sioux leaders Sitting Bull and Crazy Horse gathered almost 2,000 warriors from the Sioux, Cheyenne, and Arapaho tribes. While the warriors camped along the Little Bighorn River in Montana, the U.S. Army planned to attack them.

Before all the U.S. troops had arrived, Lieutenant Colonel George Armstrong Custer led his army unit in an attack on the Indians. During the short battle that followed, Custer and his 264 soldiers were killed.

The Plains Indians won the Battle of the Little Bighorn, but they lost many other battles. Within a few years after their victory, the Indians in Montana had moved onto reservations. A new chapter in Montana's history began.

A Sioux artist drew pictures of dead U.S. Army soldiers *(facing page)* after the Indians' victory at the Battle of the Little Bighorn. Another artist chose to show a heroic Custer *(right)* leading his men into battle.

Railroad advertisements encouraged people to move to Montana.

During the 1880s, some settlers in the Territory of Montana were growing rich from the region's minerals. Marcus Daly, a miner, became wealthy after finding copper in the mines of Anaconda and Butte Hill. Most miners were not interested in copper, but Daly and a few others understood its value. Miles and miles of copper wire were needed on the East Coast for telephone and electric lines. Daly was determined to supply it.

Railroads made Daly's wealth possible. Trains hauled copper and other minerals east for sale and returned with mining machinery. The railroads also carried the state's wheat and cattle to market. People rode trains to Montana to settle on ranches and farms.

Towns sprang up along the railroad tracks. By the late 1880s, Montana's population had reached 150,000. Many people had decided to make Montana their home, and in 1889 the U.S. government admitted Montana to the Union, making it the 41st state.

Montana's flag contains the state seal, which shows the mountain scenery that gave the state its name. This version of the flag became official in 1981.

Montana provided much of the coal needed to fuel trains.

Trains, the best mode of transportation at the turn of the century, were fueled by coal, which Montana had in abundance. In 1924 mining companies came to the town of Colstrip. Using heavy machinery, workers stripped away trees and soil to uncover the coal.

Montanans profited from mining coal until the Great Depression of the 1930s. During the depression, people throughout the country had little or no money to buy food and other necessities. As a result, factories around the United States made fewer goods or stopped manufacturing altogether.

Factories also bought less coal and other raw materials needed to make goods. With few buyers for their products, miners and loggers lost their jobs. At the same time, hot, dry weather scorched the plains. Crops and cattle died for lack of water. Farmers and ranchers abandoned their land.

During the 1930s, natural disasters such as a plague of grasshoppers ruined crops and forced people to leave the state. Sometimes whole towns left, abandoning homes, farms, and schools.

10,000 B.C. — Native Americans hunt mammoths in what is now Montana

A.D.1600 — Plains Indians begin to hunt on horseback

1804 — Lewis and Clark head west to map the Louisiana Purchase

1847 — Montana's Fort Benton is built

1864 — Montana is added to U.S. territory

1876 — Battle of the Little Bighorn

Montana's state capitol building is in Helena. In 1991, because of a decreasing population, Montana lost one of its U.S. representatives.

40

1889 Montana becomes the 41st state

1929 Montana's economy suffers with the start of the Great Depression

1951 Oil is discovered in Montana

1991 The number of U.S. representatives from Montana is cut from 2 to 1

Montana began to recover from its slump when World War II started in 1939. The U.S. government needed beef from the state's cattle ranches to feed soldiers. Factories demanded copper and coal from Montana's mines to build weapons and to fuel factories.

After the war ended in 1945, Montana's wealth grew. Oil was found in the state in the 1950s, and tons of coal were mined and sold in the 1970s. But with more drought and the loss of many mining and lumbering jobs in the 1980s, Montanans again faced hard times.

From the Indians to the miners, many strands have already been wound into Montana's history. Montanans of today continue to add their stories to the history of the state.

41

Living and Working in Montana

Alaska, Texas, and California are the only states larger than Montana, yet the Big Sky Country has fewer people than Rhode Island, the nation's smallest state. Most of Montana's 800,000 residents live in the Rocky Mountains region or in the river valleys of the Great Plains, where many miles separate ranches and towns.

Montana's small population creates problems for such a large state. Keeping miles and miles of roads in good repair is expensive. The tax money taken from the state's few residents must pay for those roads, for schools, and for other public services.

43

Many Montanans live far from big cities.

In rural areas, some students attend one-room schools.

Providing a good education for students in rural areas is difficult. Many students attend city schools. But children who live on ranches and farms sometimes share their classrooms with only a few other students. These schools usually cannot afford to offer many different classes or to buy computers.

Slightly more than half of Montana's people live in cities or large towns. Most of Montana's towns grew from small mining camps or railroad stops. The largest cities are Billings, Great Falls, Missoula, Butte, and Helena, the state capital. Billings, the largest of these cities, has about 80,000 people.

A Crow Indian girl

A German-Scot weaver at Red Lodge

Indians were the only residents of Montana until the 1800s, but now they make up 5 percent of the state's population. Seven reservations are home to most of the 37,000 Native Americans living in Montana.

About 94 percent of Montanans are white people. Many of their grandparents came from Midwestern or Southern states. Others have ancestors from European countries such as Norway, Sweden, Finland, Wales, Ireland, Germany,

Team roping at a Crow Agency rodeo

Scottish Highland fling

and Yugoslavia. The remaining 6 percent of Montanans are Asian, Hispanic, or African American.

The state's European, Native American, and other cultures are represented in community events. Performers dance to German pol-kas at Red Lodge's Festival of Nations. Indian dancers whirl trailing feathers at powwows in the towns of Browning and Crow Agency. Cowboys test their skills at rodeos such as the annual Bucking Horse Sale in Miles City.

Every year, thousands of people travel to Montana. At the Little Bighorn Battlefield National Monument, tourists explore the battlegrounds of the Little Bighorn. The Grant-Kohrs Ranch gives visitors an idea of what life was like for early cattle ranchers. On the prairie, vacationers can ride horses along trails or take covered-wagon trips.

One of the most scenic of Montana's tourist attractions is Glacier National Park. Backpackers and mountain climbers enjoy climbing Glacier's rugged mountain peaks. Skiers speed down Montana's snow-packed mountain slopes.

Rafters splash through river rapids, and fishers cast for trout in the cold mountain streams that make Montana an excellent place for fly-fishing.

Many Montanans help tourists enjoy their stay in the state. Jobs in tourism are called service jobs. There are other kinds of service jobs too. The people who load railroad cars in Billings and Great Falls have service jobs. Other service workers include teachers, doctors, salesclerks, truck drivers, and mechanics. More Montanans work in services than in any other field.

Visitors to Montana can discover the steep peaks and rushing rivers of Glacier National Park *(left)* or tour Little Bighorn Battlefield National Monument *(above)* in southern Montana.

Trucks transport freshly cut logs to sawmills and factories.

Manufacturing employs 6 percent of working Montanans. Many of the state's factories produce lumber and wood products. After cutting down evergreen trees from Montana's forests, loggers send the timber to sawmills where it is cut into boards. Factory workers in Missoula process some of the lumber into plywood or paper.

Other factories make food products or process minerals. Some food-processing plants refine sugar or mill flour. Using resources mined in Montana, some of the state's workers make metal pipe, mold bricks, or mix cement. Workers in Billings refine the state's oil.

Most of the minerals unearthed in Montana are sold to factories in other states. Oil and coal, two major sources of fuel, are Montana's most valuable minerals. Eastern Montana has the largest coal reserves in the United States. Miners also dig copper, silver, gold, and lead, primarily from southwestern Montana. The state is among the nation's top producers of these metals.

Montana's oil wells earn a lot of money for the state.

Montanans use their land to grow crops such as cherries *(above)* and to raise livestock such as sheep *(right)* and cattle *(facing page)*.

Agriculture earns only 1 percent of the state's money. About one-fourth of Montana's ranchland is used to grow crops. Because of the state's dry climate, farmers must irrigate some of this land. Wheat and barley are the state's main crops, but farmers also plant hay, potatoes, sugar beets, and cherry trees. A large number of Christmas trees grow on farms in the Rocky Mountains, and the town of Eureka claims to be the Christmas Tree Capital of the World.

Cattle ranchers still play a part in Montana's agriculture. Beef and dairy cattle and sheep graze on three-quarters of the state's farmland. Hogs are also raised. The broad, open ranges, scattered with cattle and cowboys, keep the spirit of Montana's first ranchers alive.

Open-pit mines can harm
Montana's natural
resources.

Protecting the Environment

Montana's wealth lies in its natural resources—timbered mountains, grass-covered prairies, minerals such as coal and gold, and breathtaking scenery. Many Montanans depend on these natural resources to make a living. But when some valuable resources are used, other equally valuable resources are threatened.

For example, minerals have brought money, jobs, and people to Montana for more than 100 years. But mining these resources has damaged Montana's land, water, and wildlife.

To unearth metals such as gold and copper, which are hidden in underground rocks, miners blast or dig a huge, gaping hole out of the land to create an **open-pit mine**. Miners then remove rock from the mine and separate the metals from the rock.

By creating an open-pit mine, people destroy the area's trees and grasses. People also uncover loose soil and rocks that produce acid, a harmful sour chemical. Rainwater washes the dirt and acid into nearby streams and rivers, clouding the waterways and poisoning fish and plants.

In the gold-rush days, miners used mercury to separate gold from lead rocks. The miners left behind piles of lead and mercury, which are toxic, or poisonous, metals. These wastes seeped into both surface water and **groundwater**—water below the earth's surface that is used for drinking.

Miners no longer use mercury, but new methods of mining can be just as dangerous. Gold miners now crush rocks containing small amounts of gold and then wash the rocks with cyanide. Cyanide pulls the gold from the rock. This process is called heap leaching.

Miners keep the cyanide, a highly poisonous chemical, in a pond lined with watertight plastic. But the cyanide sometimes leaks out of the pond and into groundwater. People who drink the contaminated groundwater can be poisoned.

Even if the pond doesn't leak, it is dangerous. Thirsty birds and animals see the cyanide pond and think that it holds water, not toxic chemicals. Thousands of birds have been poisoned by drinking from cyanide ponds.

HEAP LEACHING

1—Ore containing gold is mined.

5—Solution goes to the tank to be used again.

2—Ore is spread out in a heap, and a cyanide solution is sprayed over the ore. Waterproof liners under the heap and the pond help prevent the solution from leaking into the ground.

4—At the processing plant, the gold is recovered from the solution.

3—Solution and gold trickle to the bottom of the heap and are pumped to the processing plant.

Since the 1970s, Montana's legislature has passed laws that require mining companies to clean up their waste. This is done through a process called **reclamation**. For example, coal miners must rebuild the land after they have dug all the coal from a site. And gold miners must carefully collect their cyanide and dispose of it safely.

Miners sometimes use sprinklers *(top)* **loaded with toxic chemicals to separate gold from rock. When the site is to be abandoned, the land is reclaimed** *(bottom)*.

State workers hope to reclaim abandoned mines like this one in Zortman, Montana.

State laws have helped to protect Montana's landscape from further damage, but the laws do not deal with old abandoned mines or open-pit mines. State workers are trying to reclaim old mines, but the project is huge. More than 3,000 abandoned mines exist.

Reclaiming open-pit mines is expensive. If Montana forced companies to reclaim open-pit mines, the companies might go to a state where the cost of mining was lower. So companies are allowed to leave the craters open, exposing loose soil and acidic rocks for years to come.

59

As the dangers of careless mining become clear, more and more mining companies are cleaning up after themselves. Some miners refill open pits with the rocks and soil taken out earlier and then plant trees and grasses. Other miners cover cyanide pools with nets to keep wildlife out or use closed storage tanks instead of exposed pools.

Even Montanans who aren't miners can help protect their state's resources. Reporting signs of polluted water, such as dead fish or bad-tasting drinking water, is one way to help. Asking the government to pass laws to reclaim open-pit mines is another way to help. Montanans can make sure that the wealth and beauty of their state is protected.

Montana's Famous People

◀ GARY COOPER

ACTORS & ARTISTS

Gary Cooper (1901–1961) was once a guide in Yellowstone National Park but is more famous for his career as an actor. Born in Helena, Montana, Cooper appeared in more than 90 movies and won Academy Awards for his performances in *Sergeant York* and *High Noon.*

Charles Marion Russell (1865–1926) worked as a hunter and a cowboy in the Territory of Montana before becoming a full-time artist. Russell's drawings, paintings, and sculptures capture the spirit of life on the western frontier.

CHARLES M. RUSSELL ▶

◀ DAVE McNALLY

▼ JOHN BOZEMAN

ATHLETE

Dave McNally (born 1942), a baseball player from Billings, Montana, pitched for the Baltimore Orioles during the 1960s and 1970s. During his career, McNally helped the Orioles win 184 games. In 1970 he became the first pitcher to hit a grand slam in the World Series.

EXPLORERS & SCIENTISTS

John Bozeman (1835–1867) headed west with gold seekers in 1862. He blazed a trail that led directly to Montana's mining camps. The city of Bozeman, Montana, carries the explorer's name.

John R. Horner (born 1946), a native of Shelby, Montana, found the first dinosaur nests ever uncovered. The nests held hundreds of dinosaur eggs and the bones of baby dinosaurs.

Yellowstone Kelly (1849–1928) led fur traders and pioneers through Montana. Born Luther Sage Kelly in New York, the guide was nicknamed Yellowstone because he was an expert scout in the Yellowstone River valley.

◄ JOHN R. HORNER

◄ CHIEF DULL KNIFE

JANINE PEASE-WINDY BOY ►

◄ CHIEF PLENTY COUPS

NATIVE AMERICAN LEADERS

Chief Dull Knife (1810?–1883?), also known as Morning Star, was a leader of the Northern Cheyenne people. After the tribe was moved from Montana to a reservation in Oklahoma, Dull Knife helped his people return to their Montana hunting grounds. Indians on the Northern Cheyenne Reservation in Montana now call themselves the Morning Star People in Dull Knife's honor.

Janine Pease–Windy Boy (born 1949) is president of the Little Big Horn College in Crow Agency, Montana. She works to preserve the culture of the Crow Indians and to improve education for all Native Americans.

Chief Plenty Coups (1849?–1932) helped the Crow Indians keep some of their land in Montana by carefully planning treaties with the U.S. government. Plenty Coups worked closely with white people but practiced the traditions of the Crow.

63

Robert Yellowtail (1889–1988) became the first Indian superintendent of the Crow Indian Reservation in 1934. Under his leadership, which lasted for 50 years, the Crow Indians managed reservation affairs for the first time.

MINERS & RANCHERS

William A. Clark (1839–1925) and Marcus Daly (1841–1900) are sometimes called the Copper Kings because both men became wealthy from their copper mines in Montana. Clark and Daly were also politically active.

▲ WILLIAM A. CLARK

▲ MARCUS DALY

Richard Grant (1794–1862) set up the first ranch in Montana. Grant made a practice of trading one of his healthy cows for two tired and weak cows herded by pioneers traveling the Oregon Trail. Grant then fattened the weak cattle on Montana's rich pastures.

Granville Stuart (1834–1918) was one of the first miners to discover gold in Montana, but his main interest was raising cattle. Stuart was involved in Montana politics and spent his later years writing about the state's history.

◀ GRANVILLE STUART

◀ DOLLY SMITH CUSKER AKERS

POLITICAL LEADERS

Dolly Smith Cusker Akers (1901–1986), who grew up in Wolf Point, Montana, was the first Assiniboin Indian woman to lead the Fort Peck tribal governing board. In 1932 Akers became the first woman and the first Indian to be elected to the Montana state legislature.

Michael J. Mansfield (born 1903), raised in Great Falls, Montana, was a miner, college professor, and politician. He served for many years in the U.S. House of Representatives and in the U.S. Senate. From 1977 to 1989, Mansfield was the U.S. ambassador to Japan.

Jeannette Rankin (1880–1973), born in Missoula, Montana, was the first woman elected to the U.S. Congress. Rankin worked to get government funds to help support poor women and their children.

◀ A. B. GUTHRIE, JR.

MICHAEL J. MANSFIELD ▶

JEANNETTE RANKIN ▶

WRITERS & JOURNALISTS

A. B. Guthrie, Jr. (1901–1991), set many of his novels and stories in Montana, his home state. He also wrote many scripts for western films, including *Shane*. In 1950 Guthrie won a Pulitzer Prize for his book *The Way West*.

Chet Huntley (1911–1974) was born in Cardwell, Montana. He worked as a reporter for three major television networks—ABC, CBS, and NBC—before anchoring the "Huntley-Brinkley Report," a nightly television news program.

Dorothy M. Johnson (1905–1984) grew up in Montana. Her books tell the history of the American West. The movies *The Man Who Shot Liberty Valence* and *A Man Called Horse* are based on Johnson's stories.

DOROTHY M. ▶
JOHNSON

65

Facts-at-a-Glance

Nickname: Treasure State
Song: "Montana"
Motto: *Oro y Plata* (Gold and Silver)
Flower: bitterroot
Tree: ponderosa pine
Bird: western meadowlark

Population: 799,065*
Rank in population, nationwide: 44th
Area: 147,046 sq mi (380,848 sq km)
Rank in area, nationwide: 4th
Date and ranking of statehood:
   November 8, 1889, the 41st state
Capital: Helena
Major cities (and populations*):
   Billings (81,151), Great Falls (55,097),
   Missoula (42,918), Butte-Silver Bow (33,336),
   Helena (24,569)
U.S. senators: 2
U.S. representatives: 1
Electoral votes: 3

*1990 census

Places to visit: Glacier National Park in northwestern Montana, Medicine Rocks near Ekalaka, Virginia City near Dillon, Little Bighorn Battlefield National Monument, Bozeman Museum of the Rockies

Annual events: Whoop-up Days in Conrad (May), Music Festival in Red Lodge (June), North American Indian Days in Browning (July), Wild Horse Stampede Rodeo in Wolf Point (July), State Fair and Rodeo in Great Falls (Aug.)

Average January temperature: 18° F (–8° C)   **Average July temperature:** 68° F (20° C)

Natural resources: soil, coal, oil, natural gas, gold, lumber, sand and gravel

Agricultural products: beef, wheat, hay, barley, milk, sugar beets

Manufactured goods: lumber and wood products, petroleum and coal products, printed materials, clay and glass products

ENDANGERED SPECIES
Mammals—black-footed ferret, gray wolf
Birds—peregrine falcon, whooping crane, bald eagle

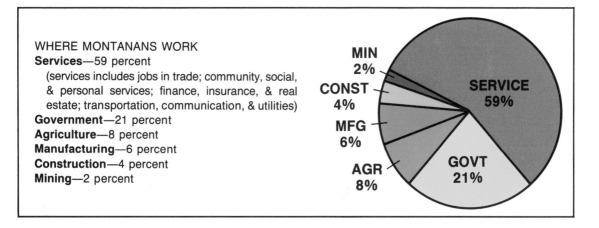

WHERE MONTANANS WORK
Services—59 percent
  (services includes jobs in trade; community, social, & personal services; finance, insurance, & real estate; transportation, communication, & utilities)
Government—21 percent
Agriculture—8 percent
Manufacturing—6 percent
Construction—4 percent
Mining—2 percent

MIN 2%
CONST 4%
MFG 6%
AGR 8%
SERVICE 59%
GOVT 21%

67

PRONUNCIATION GUIDE

Anaconda (an-uh-KAHN-duh)

Arapaho (uh-RAP-uh-hoh)

Assiniboin (uh-SIHN-uh-boyn)

Butte (BYOOT)

Cheyenne (shy-AN)

Gros Ventre (GROH vahnt)

Helena (HEHL-uh-nuh)

Kalispel (KAL-uh-spehl)

Kootenai (KOOT-ihn-ay)

Missoula (muh-ZOO-luh)

Sioux (SOO)

Glossary

groundwater Water that lies beneath the earth's surface. The water comes from rain and snow that seep through soil into the cracks and other openings in rocks. Groundwater supplies wells and springs.

irrigation Watering land by directing water through canals, ditches, pipes, or sprinklers.

open-pit mine A large hole created to get at metals lying near the earth's surface.

prairie A large area of level or gently rolling grassy land with few trees.

precipitation Rain, snow, hail and other forms of moisture that fall to earth.

reclamation The process of rebuilding land that has been mined and making it usable again for plants, animals, or people.

reservation Public land set aside by the government to be used by Native Americans.

reservoir A place where water is collected and stored for later use.

treaty An agreement between two or more groups, usually having to do with peace or trade.

69

Index

Acknowledgments:

Maryland Cartographics, Inc., pp. 2, 11; Montana Power Company, pp. 2–3, 14–15, 51; Jack Lindstrom, p. 6; The Montana Historical Society, pp. 7, 24, 25, 27, 28 (left, center, and right), 30, 33, 38, 64 (center); Kent and Donna Dannen, pp. 8, 13 (top and bottom right), 49 (top right); Travel Montana, G. Wiltsie, p. 9; Travel Montana, G. Wunderwald, p. 40; Travel Montana, D. Scott, p. 53; Travel Montana, Kis, p. 69; Michael Crummet, pp. 10, 19, 45, 46 (right and left), 47 (right and left), 52 (right), 58 (top), 59, 60, 68; Jerg Kroener, pp. 13 (bottom left), 54, 71; Gerry Lemmo, pp. 16, 44; © Crystal Images, 1992, Kathleen Marie Menke, pp. 17, 50; H. L. James, Montana Bureau of Mines and Geology, p. 18; Independent Picture Service, pp. 21, 22, 62 (top and bottom right), 63 (center left), 64 (top right and left); United States National Park Service-Warren Collection, p. 29; Patrick Cone, pp. 32, 42–43; The Southwest Museum, Los Angeles (photo #CT.1), p. 34; Library of Congress, p. 35; Chicago Historical Society (negative #11), p. 36; Museum of the Rockies, Montana State University, pp. 39, 63 (top); Theresa Early, p. 49 (left); Montana Cooperative Extension Service, p. 52 (left); Bryan Liedahl, p. 57; Robin McCulloch, Montana Bureau of Mines and Geology, p. 58 (bottom); Betty Groskin, Photo Agent: Jeff Greenberg, p. 61; Hollywood Book & Poster Co., p. 62 (top left); National Baseball Hall of Fame Museum, p. 62 (bottom left); Kyle Brehm, p. 63 (center right); Smithsonian Institution (photo #3405), p. 63 (bottom); Alvina C. Welliver, p. 64 (bottom); Maureen and Mike Mansfield Library, University of Montana, p. 65 (top right and left); Stuart S. White, Great Falls *Tribune*, p. 65 (bottom left); Stan Paregien, p. 65 (bottom right); Jean Matheny, p. 66.